I Can L

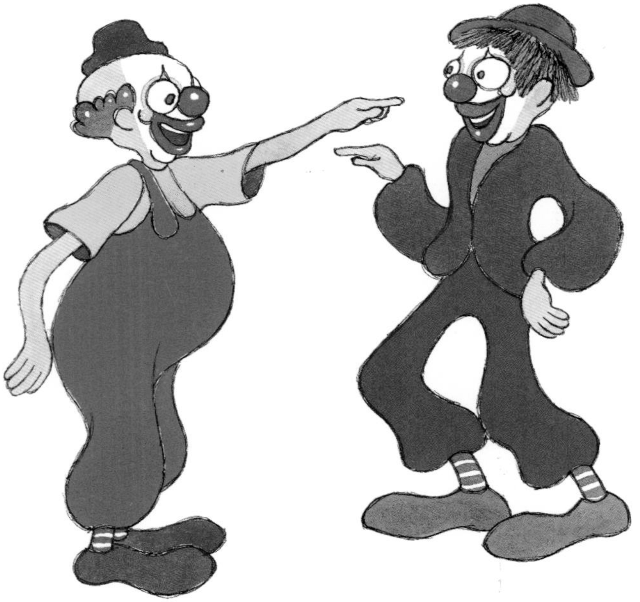

Illustrated by Ireen Denton

Rigby

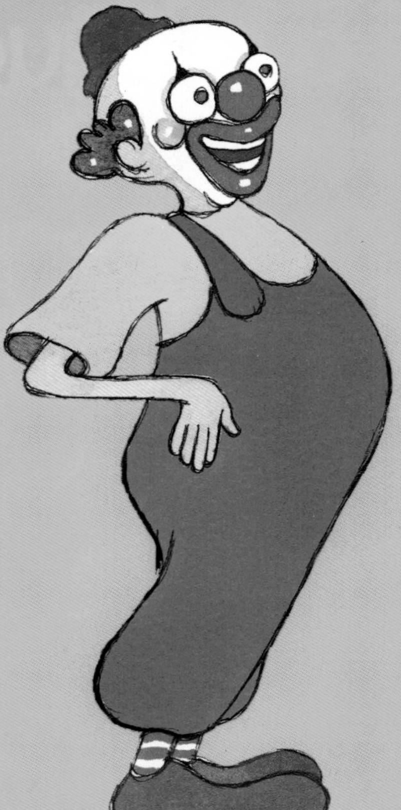

I can laugh.

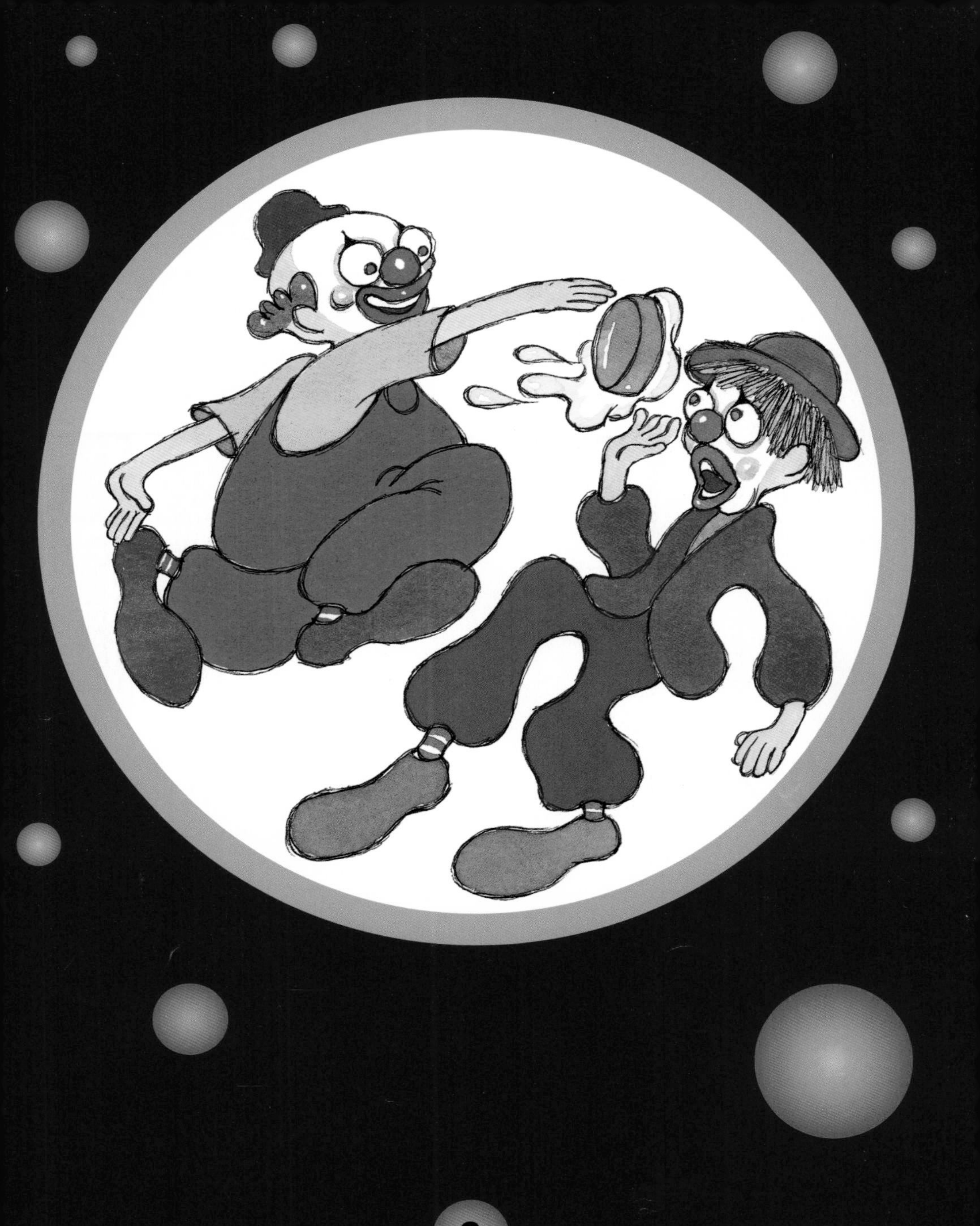

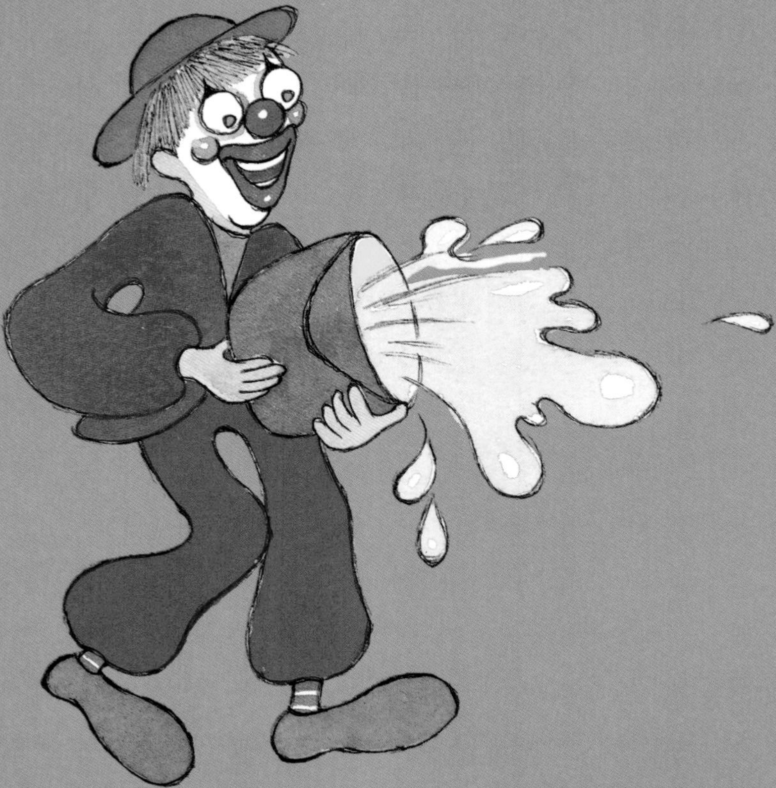

I can laugh.

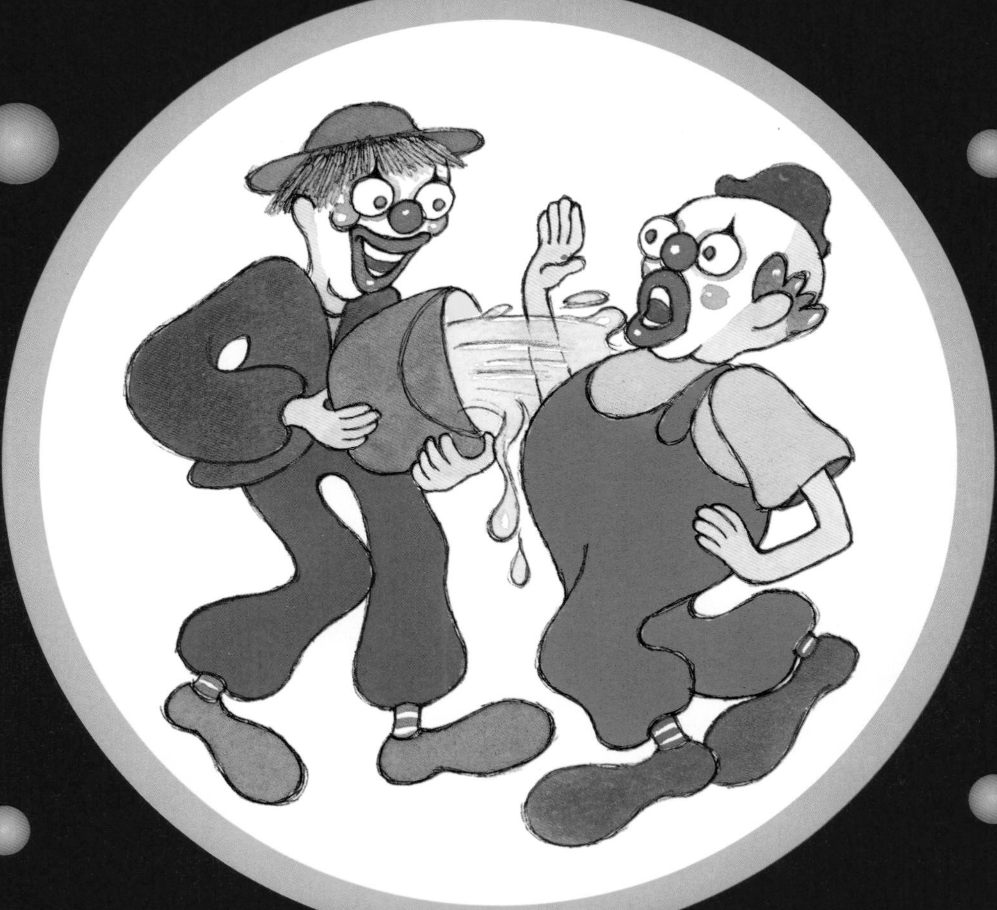

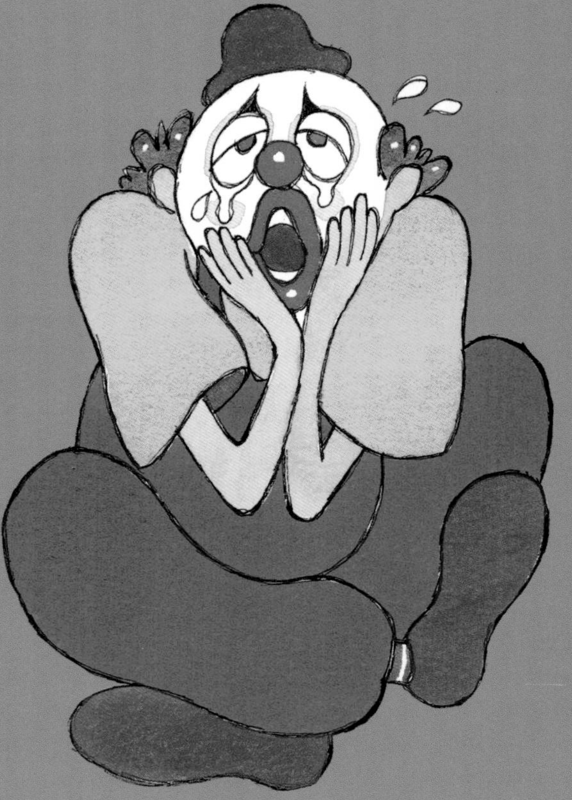

I can cry.

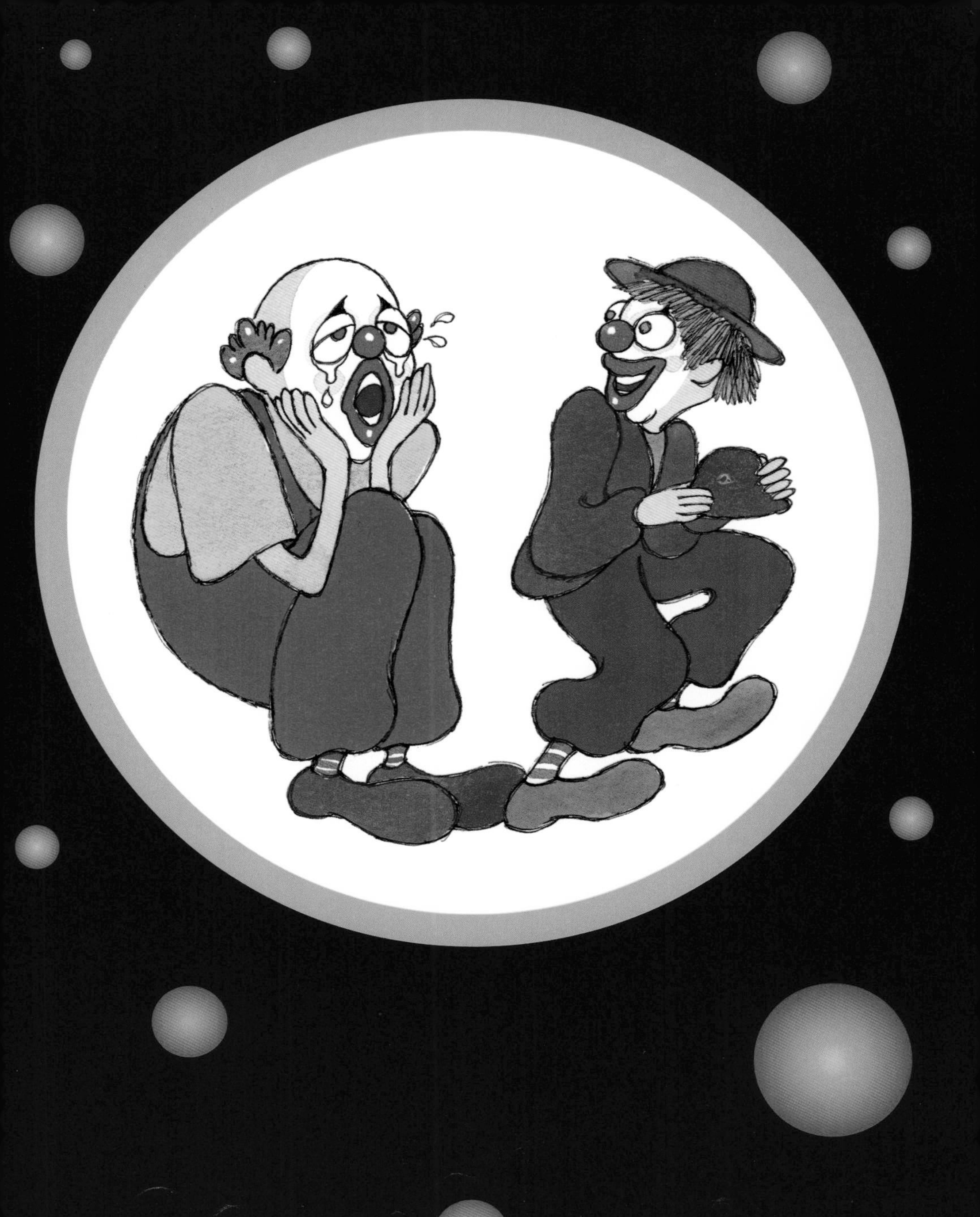

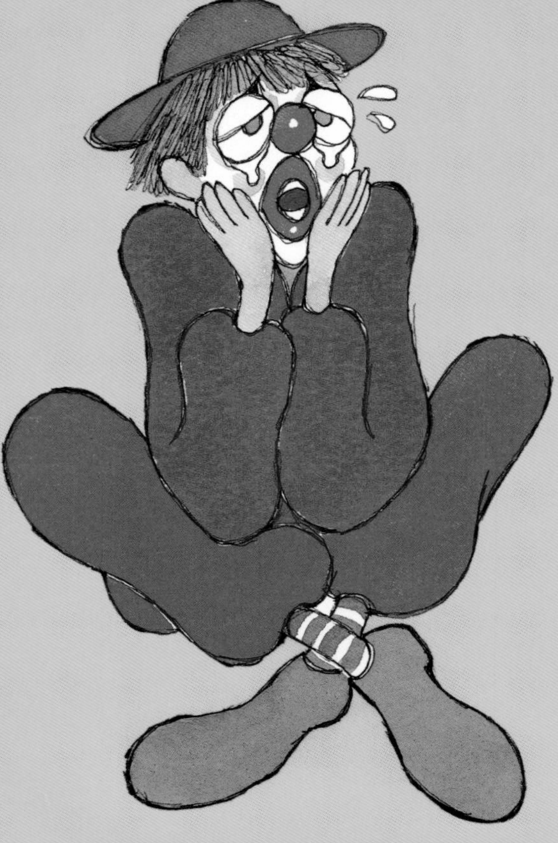

I can cry.

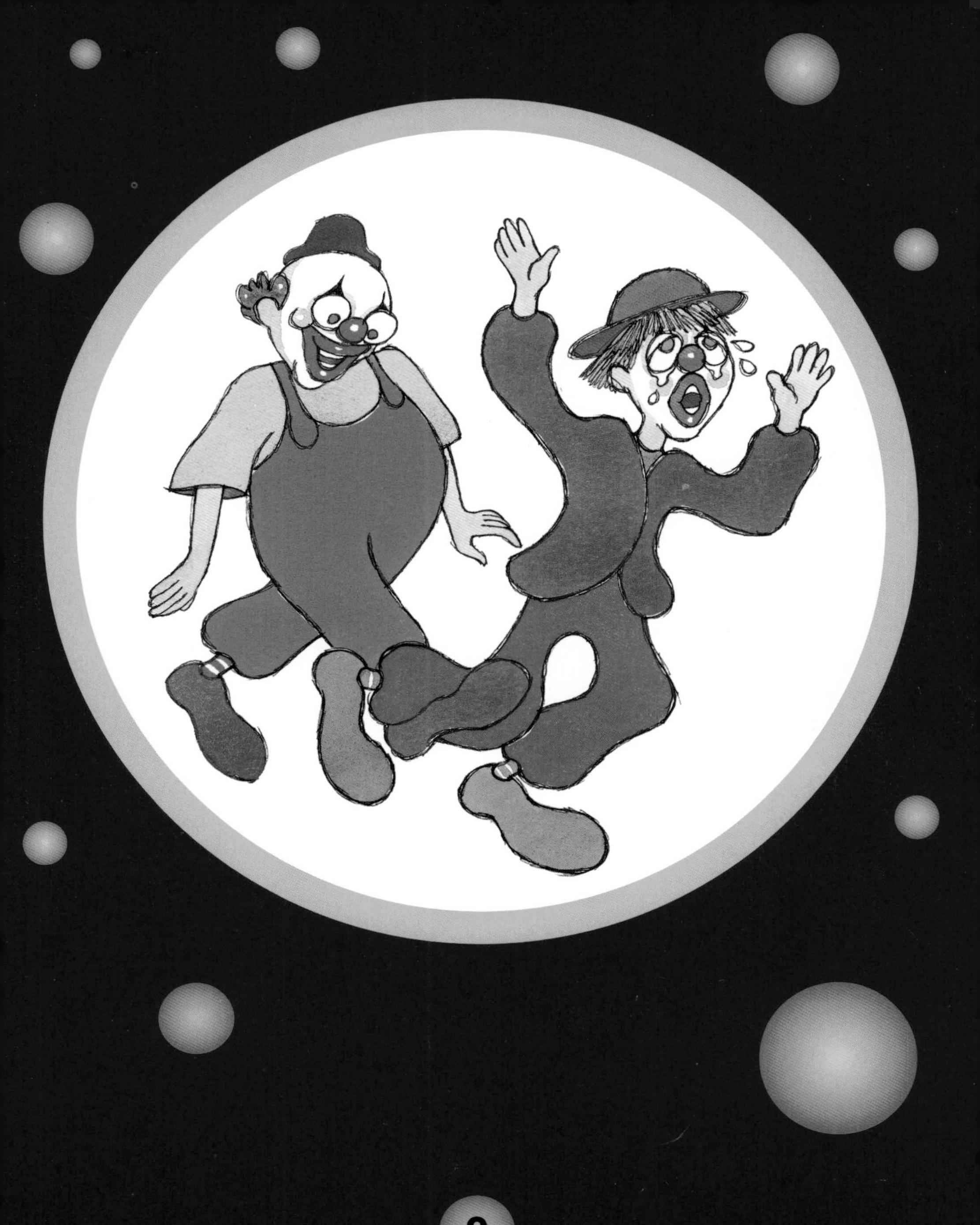

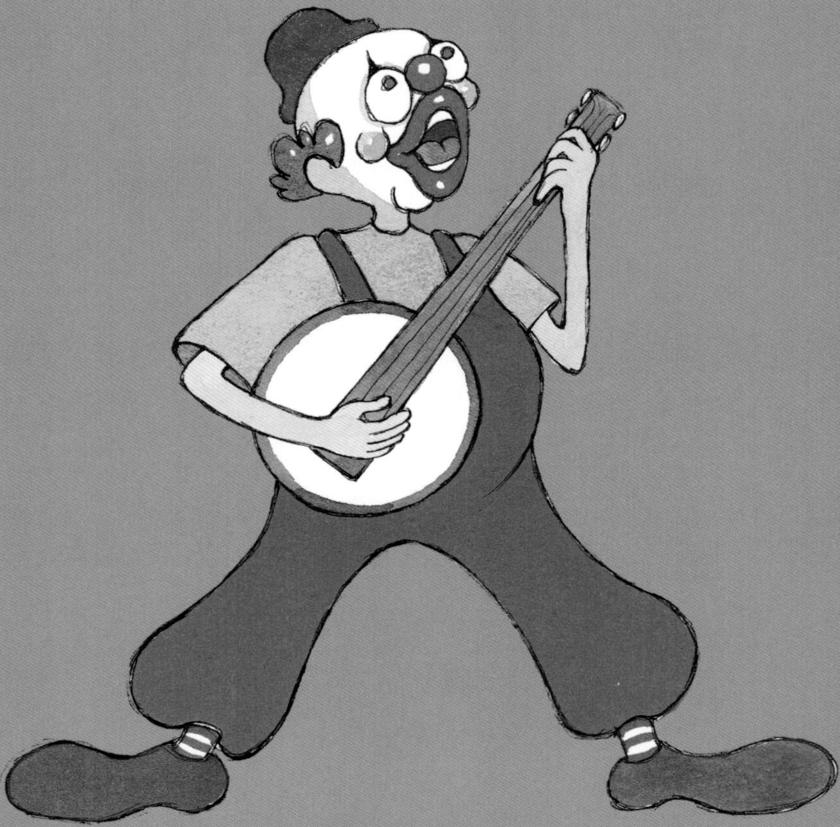

I can sing.

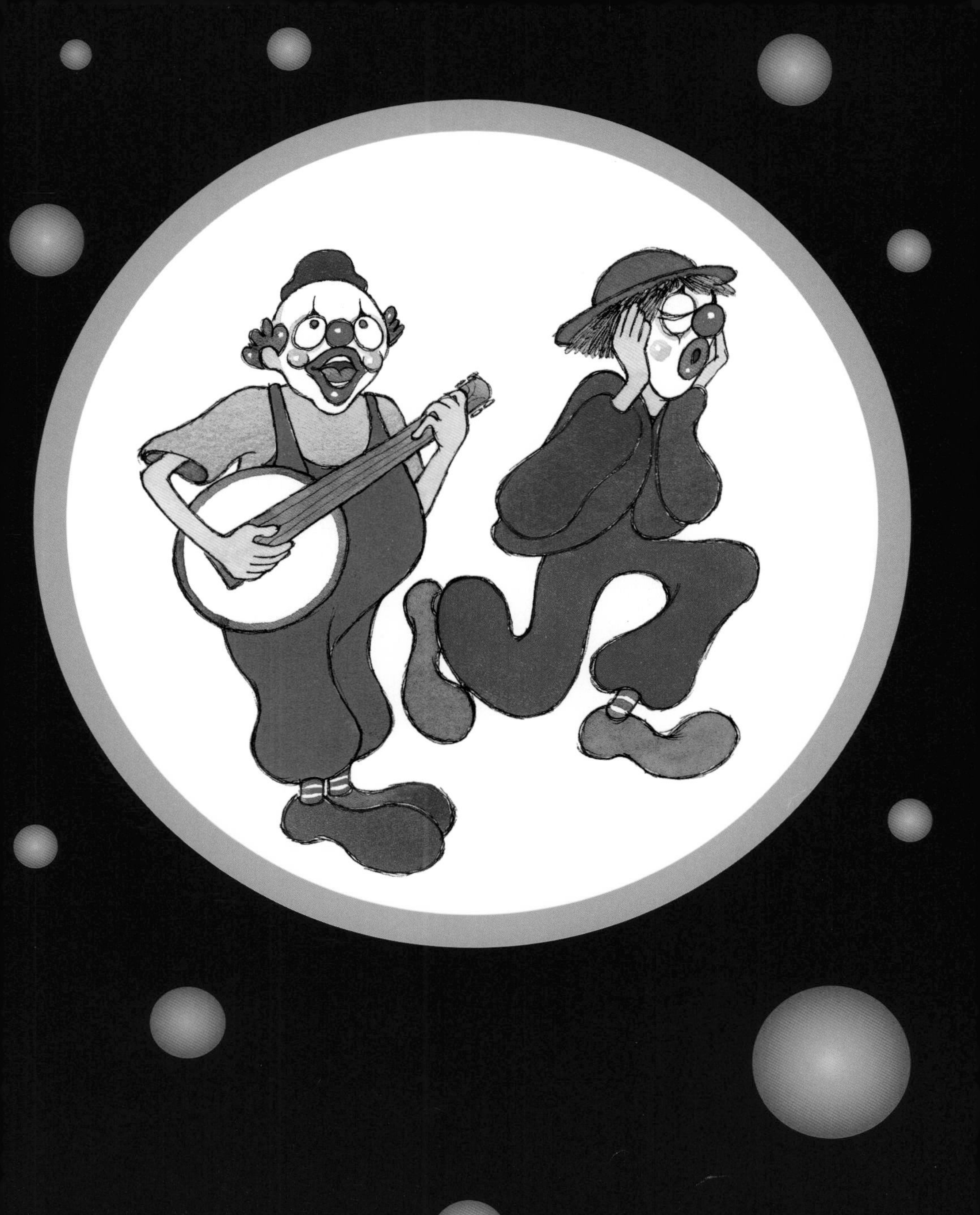

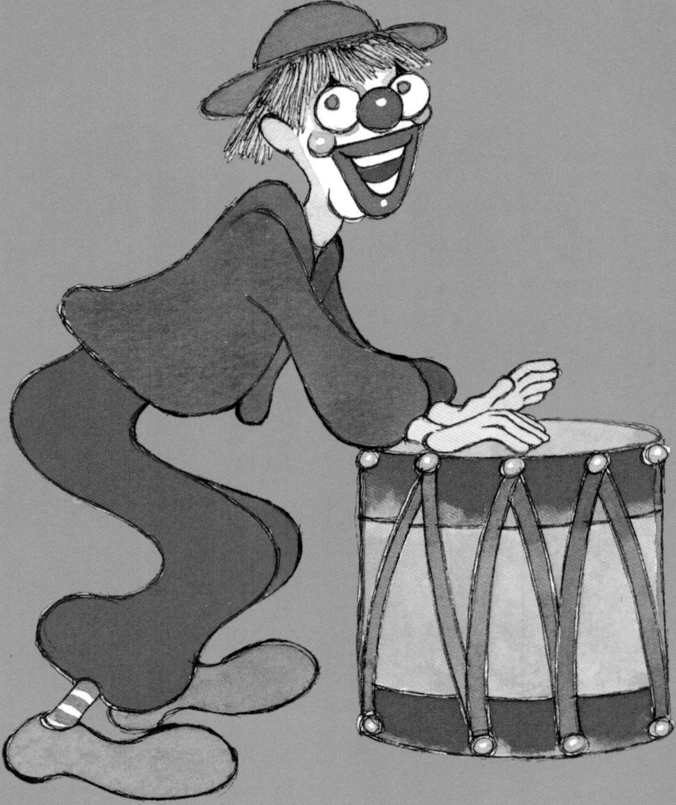

I can sing.

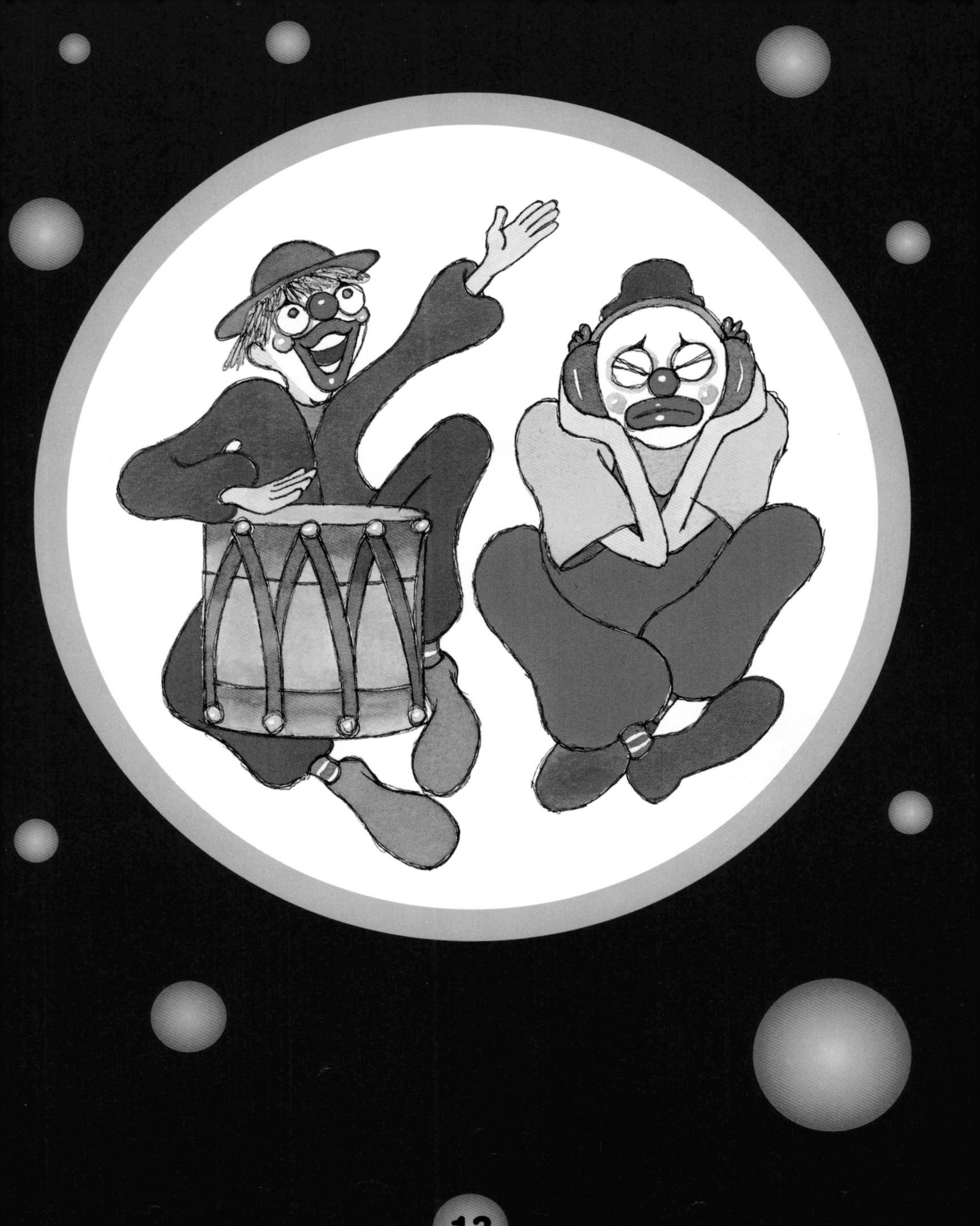

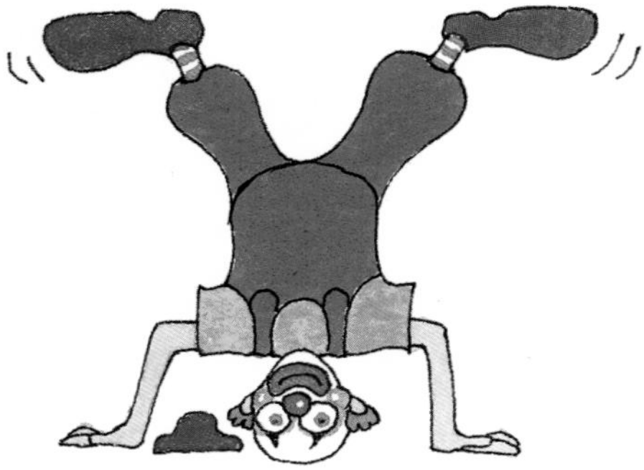

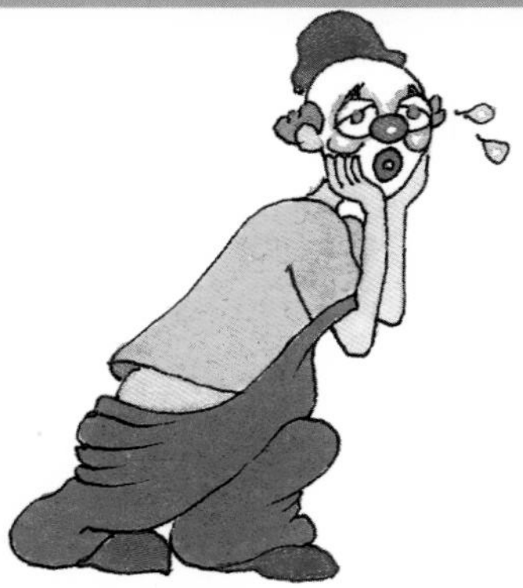

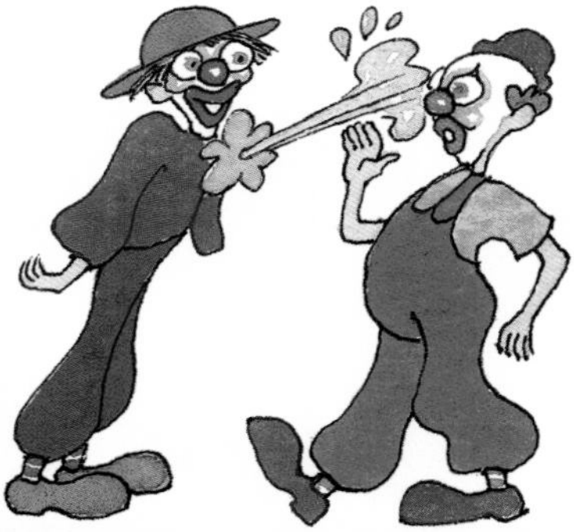

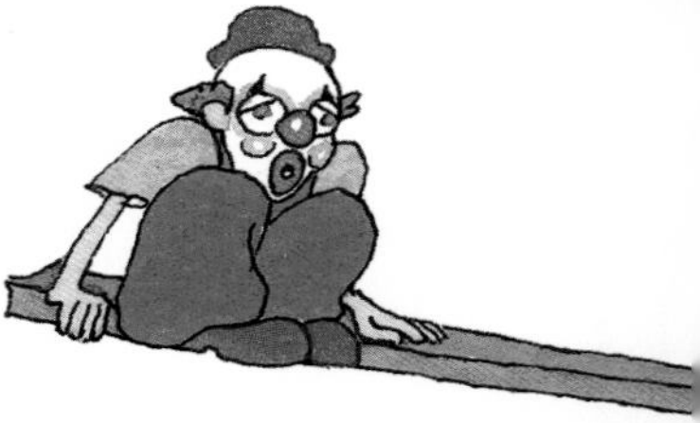

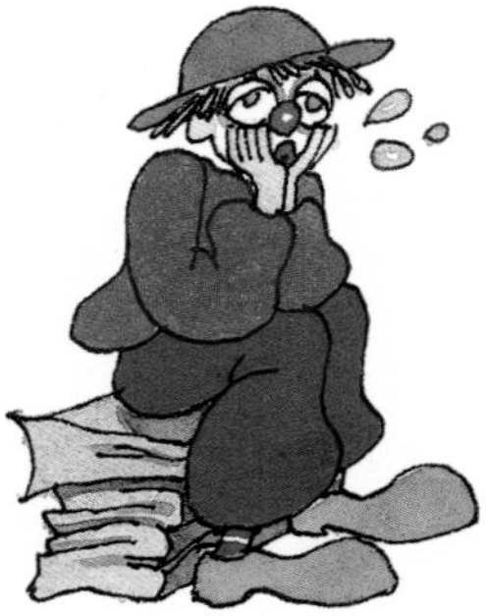

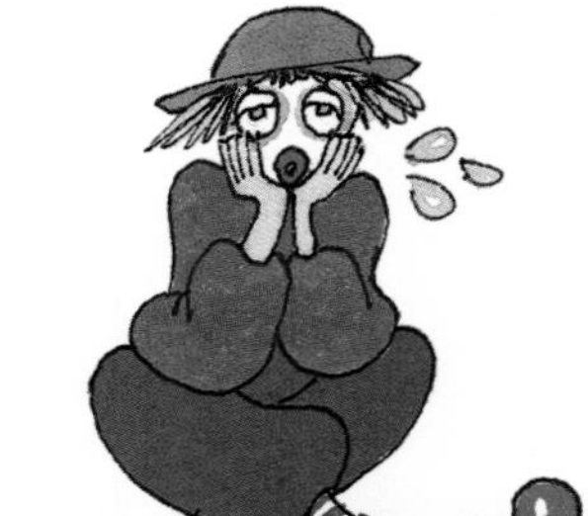

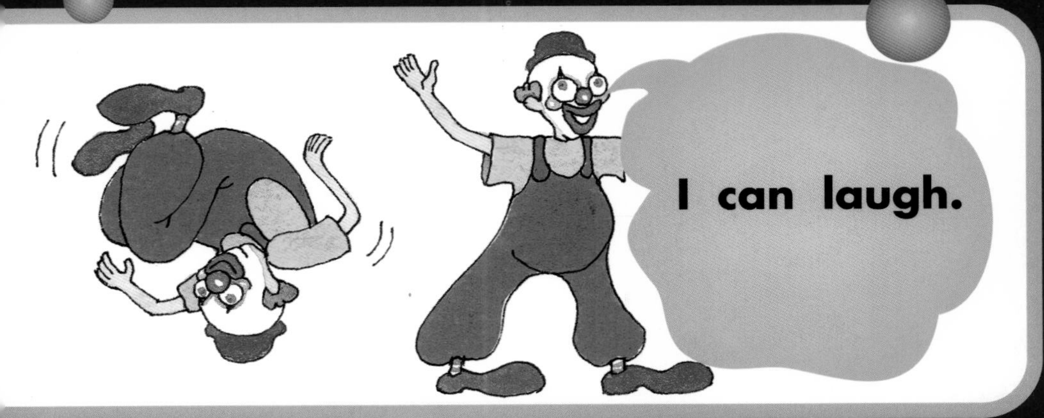
I can laugh.

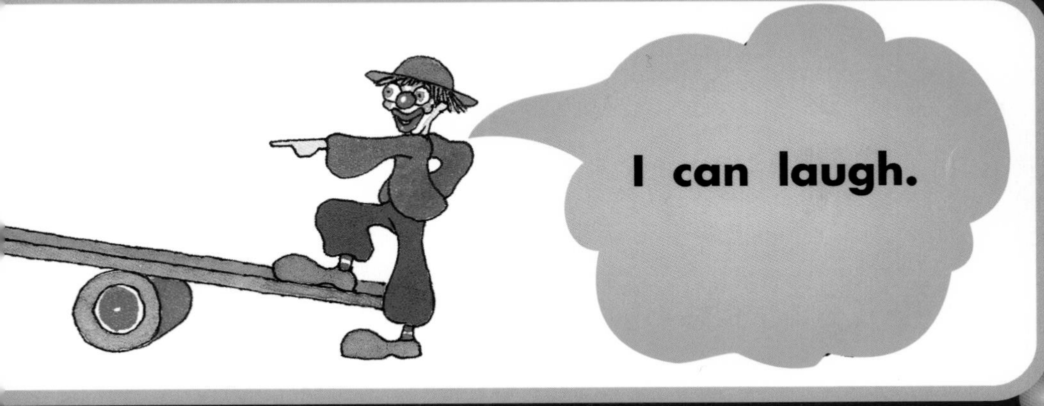
I can laugh.

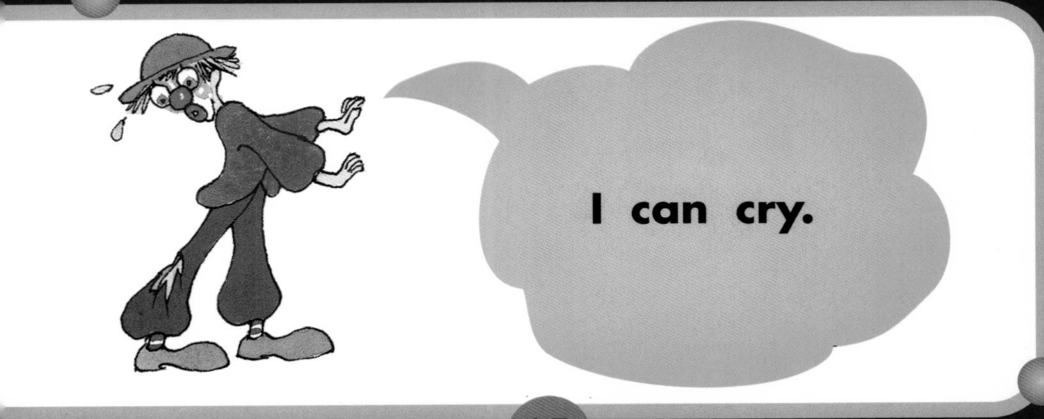
I can cry.

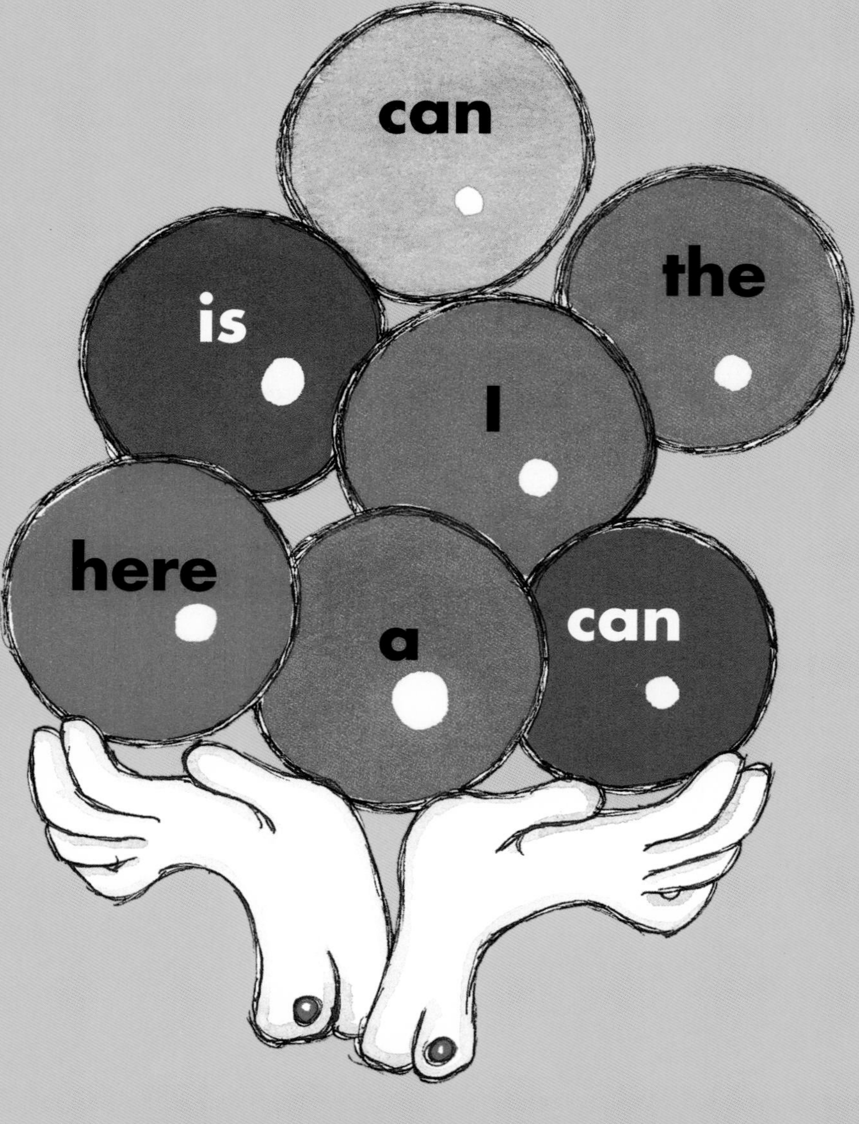
can
the
is
I
here
a
can